margaret Tempest.

HARE JOINS THE HOME GUARD

Uniform with this volume:

SQUIRREL GOES SKATING
WISE OWL'S STORY
LITTLE GREY RABBIT'S PARTY
THE KNOT SQUIRREL TIED
FUZZYPEG GOES TO SCHOOL
LITTLE GREY RABBIT'S CHRISTMAS
MOLDY WARP THE MOLE
HARE JOINS THE HOME GUARD
LITTLE GREY RABBIT'S WASHING DAY
WATER RAT'S PICNIC
LITTLE GREY RABBIT'S BIRTHDAY
THE SPECKLEDY HEN
LITTLE GREY RABBIT TO THE RESCUE
LITTLE GREY RABBIT AND THE WEASELS
GREY RABBIT AND THE WANDERING
    HEDGEHOG
LITTLE GREY RABBIT MAKES LACE
HARE AND THE EASTER EGGS
LITTLE GREY RABBIT'S VALENTINE
LITTLE GREY RABBIT'S PAINT BOX
GREY RABBIT FINDS A SHOE
GREY RABBIT AND THE CIRCUS
GREY RABBIT'S MAY DAY
HARE GOES SHOPPING
LITTLE GREY RABBIT'S PANCAKE DAY
LITTLE GREY RABBIT GOES TO THE NORTH
    POLE
FUZZYPEG'S BROTHER

LITTLE GREY RABBIT'S PAINTING BOOK

LITTLE GREY RABBIT'S SONG BOOK
Words by Alison Uttley
Music by David Davis
Published by Ascherberg, Hopwood & Crew Ltd.
16 Mortimer Street, London W.1.

Hare
Joins the
Home Guard

by Alison Uttley
Pictures by
Margaret Tempest

Collins, 14 St. James's Place London

First Impression 1941
Fifth Impression 1970
Sixth Impression 1972

ISBN 0 00 194108 9

PRINTED IN GREAT BRITAIN
COLLINS CLEAR-TYPE PRESS: LONDON AND GLASGOW

FOREWORD

OF course you must understand that Grey Rabbit's home had no electric light or gas, and even the candles were made from pith of rushes dipped in wax from the wild bees' nests, which Squirrel found. Water there was in plenty, but it did not come from a tap. It flowed from a spring outside, which rose up from the ground and went to a brook. Grey Rabbit cooked on a fire, but it was a wood fire, there was no coal in that part of the country. Tea did not come from India, but from a little herb known very well to country people, who once dried it and used it in their cottage homes. Bread was baked from wheat ears, ground fine, and Hare and Grey Rabbit gleaned in the cornfields to get the wheat.

The doormats were plaited rushes, like country-made mats, and cushions were stuffed with wool gathered from the hedges where sheep pushed through the thorns. As for the looking-glass, Grey Rabbit found the glass, dropped from a lady's handbag, and Mole made a frame for it. Usually the animals gazed at themselves in the still pools as so many country children have done. The country ways of Grey Rabbit were the country ways known to the author.

SQUIRREL AND HARE sat at the table waiting for breakfast. The toast was made and the kettle was boiling on the fire. Little Grey Rabbit warmed the tea-pot and put in three spoonfuls of daisy tea. She poured the boiling water over it and placed it on the table under the tea-cosy. Then she gave Hare a big bunch of lettuce, and Squirrel a middle-sized bunch, and on her own plate she put a very little bunch of leaves. There was brown bread, and honey and nuts, and a pat of yellow butter from the Alderney cow.

"WHERE'S THE MILK, Grey Rabbit?" asked Hare. "We can't drink tea without milk."

He munched his lettuce noisily and frowned at Grey Rabbit.

"Where's Old Hedgehog?" asked Squirrel, delicately cracking a nut.

"I'll see if he's coming," said Grey Rabbit. "He has never been as late as this. Something must have happened. I hope Fuzzypeg is all right."

8

"OH, FUZZYPEG was rolling down the field like a fat little barrel last night," cried Hare. "There's nothing the matter with that young fellow."

Grey Rabbit ran to the door and looked about her. Then she spied Hedgehog the milkman. He was trotting quickly along the lane with his cans of milk. His spotted scarf fluttered in the wind and his white smock billowed behind him like a sail.

"Good-morning, Hedgehog," called Grey Rabbit, and she went to meet him.

THE MILKMAN stamped up the path and looked through the doorway at Squirrel and Hare. He put down the milk cans and waited for Grey Rabbit to get her jug.

"Have you heard the news?" he asked importantly.

"What news?" asked Hare, and he held up his empty mug. "Where's the milk, Hedgehog? We want milk, not news."

"There nearly was no milk. Nearly was never a drop," replied Hedgehog crossly. He filled Grey Rabbit's jug and then stood gazing very sternly at all of them.

"WHAT'S THE MATTER, dear Hedgehog?" asked Grey Rabbit anxiously.

"There's a war," said Hedgehog. "That's what's the matter. A war!"

"A war? What's that?" asked Hare, and they all looked puzzled.

"A war's a battle coming on us. Yes! Cows was that upset they kicked over my bucket when I told 'em and toppled me over, and I had to begin milking all over again."

"Why were the cows upset?" asked Grey Rabbit.

"AND THE MILK UPSET?" asked Hare.

"And you upset?" asked Squirrel.

"Because there's a war! Bang! Bang! Cows don't like a noise."

"Who is going to make a noise?" asked Grey Rabbit.

"Nay, I don't know. Somebody's on the war-path. I'm off to find out. Keep indoors and mind yourselves. Don't get hurted. Good-day to you all."

Hedgehog took up his pail and trotted down the path.

SQUIRREL, HARE and Little Grey Rabbit all talked at once as they sipped their tea, and ate their crisp lettuce and toast.

"Perhaps it's a Fox or a Billy-goat or a Weasel on the war-path," said Hare.

"Perhaps it's a Wolf," faltered Squirrel.

"Or a mad Bull," went on Hare cheerfully.

Tap! Rat-a-tap-tap! There was a flutter of wings and Robin the Postman appeared on the doorstep with his bag on his back.

HE HELD OUT a leafy letter to
Grey Rabbit.

"Have you heard the news?" he
asked.

"Yes. There's a war," cried the
three friends all together. "Tell us
about it, Robin."

"It's a war of Weasels. There's an
army of them coming to attack us.
You'd better get ready. They are
coming through the far-away woods to
invade our peaceful little land."

16

HE SHOOK HIS POST-BAG and showed them all the leaves which brimmed it.

"All these letters to deliver this morning," he boasted. "Everybody's got a letter to-day. We've all got to wake up and arm ourselves with spears and arrows against the invading Weasels."

Away he flew, and out of his bag frisked the letters, dropping into holes in the bank, fluttering through green doorways and open windows, telling the animal world that the Weasels were coming and that they must fight them.

"DEAR! DEAR!" cried Squirrel. "I shall fight with these." She picked up her knitting needles and began to knit a stocking at a great rate.

"Pooh!" scoffed Hare. "They won't sit waiting while you dance up to them on tiptoes with your knitting-needles, Squirrel. They'll gobble you up. Now, I shall use my catapult. Then I needn't go too close to their sharp teeth."

Grey Rabbit was staring at the little crooked words which were traced on the leaf.

"LET ME LOOK," said Squirrel, and she turned it about and peered at the writing.

"It's one of the oak leaves from Dark Wood. I wonder who sent it!"

"It's a bird's beak-writing," said Grey Rabbit. "Only a bird could scribble like this. It's a yellow-hammer's writing, I declare! Yellow-hammers are called scribbling-larks, you know."

"Of course. They write on their eggs to warn folk away, don't they?"

HARE LEANED OVER and shook his head at the tiny scrawled letters.

"I wish I were a scholar like you, Grey Rabbit. I can't read those long words. What does it say?"

"Courage! Fight for Freedom." Grey Rabbit read the letters slowly.

"Courage!" echoed Hare. "I'll learn those Weasels! I defeated the Fox, and Grey Rabbit caught the King of the Weasels, and Squirrel tied a knot in Rat's tail. We three can face an army of Weasels."

THEY HAD FINISHED washing up the breakfast things and were making the beds when there was a pitter-patter of little feet at the door.

" Goodness me! The enemy is here!" shrieked Hare, and he and Squirrel dived under their beds, leaving Grey Rabbit to face the army.

She peeped through the keyhole, and there stood her old friends, Moldy Warp and Water Rat, with a company of timid rabbits and squirrels from the woods.

" We've come to hold a council of war," said Moldy Warp, and he rapped on the door.

"WHO GOES THERE?" called Squirrel in a faint squeak.

"Friend or foe?" called Hare in a thin, high voice.

"It's Moldy Warp the Mole," laughed Grey Rabbit, and she flung wide the door and ran to welcome him.

There wasn't room inside for so many, so they sat in the garden and held council.

"The Weasels are on the war-path," said Moldy Warp.

"Where is the war-path?" asked the rabbits.

"IT'S THAT LONG LANE, the old Roman road, which runs through the woods to the hills, as straight as an arrow. That's the war-path. It comes close to your house, Grey Rabbit. The army will march down here."

Mrs. Hedgehog and her husband came hurrying up, and the Speckledy Hen bustled through the gate with a loud cluck. She was helping Fuzzypeg to carry a basket of eggs.

"WE'VE BROUGHT AMMUNI-
TION," said Fuzzypeg, pant-
ing up the path.

"We've brought these to throw at
the Weasels."

"These are old-laid eggs," explained
the Speckledy Hen. "The Hen-that-
always-lays-astray left them long ago
in the hedge."

"Capital!" cried the Mole. "They
will be deadly! Bring more if you can,
Speckledy Hen."

He looked round at the company of
excited, quivering little animals.

"HARE! You shall be the Home Guard! You must defend Grey Rabbit's house and all our homes with your life."

Hare shivered, but he drew himself up proudly.

"I'm used to being the Home Guard," said he. "I always put the key under the doormat."

"Squirrel," said Mole, turning to the little knitter. "You must knit socks and stockings and mittens and scarves for all our fighters."

Squirrel nodded, and clicked her needles.

"Grey Rabbit! You must be a nurse and take care of the wounded," said Mole.

"WHAT ABOUT ME?" asked Hedgehog. "I may be old, but I can fight. I once killed an adder with my prickles."

"You are a brave fellow, Hedgehog," nodded Mole. "I shall want you to be a leader, a captain. Water Rat will guard the river banks. Wise Owl will fly over the woods and watch for the approach of the enemy. All the rest of the animals will be fighters, hidden on the war-path with bows and arrows, with pop-guns and swords and daggers."

The rabbits whispered and nudged each other, each one eager to make his little weapon.

27

"WILL THERE BE anything to eat?" asked Hare.

"The Weasels will do the eating if we don't stop their advance," replied Moldy Warp, coolly. "We must rid our land of these pests before we think of eating."

"I thought there would be sandwiches provided," said Hare sorrowfully. "I can't fight on an empty stomach."

"I'll make you some sandwiches, Hare," whispered Grey Rabbit.

Just then a crow came cawing to the garden.

"THEY'RE COMING AFAR OFF, Moldy Warp. They are marching down the Roman lane, sweeping everything before them, eating everybody in the path. They will be here before the sun gets over the sky."

A shiver of excitement went round the circle.

"Every animal to his post," commanded Mole. "Get ready to meet these invaders and turn them back to their own wild land."

Away they all rushed to find weapons and to carry out Mole's secret plan.

THE MICE CUT sharp thorns from the hawthorns and made barricades across the war-path. The rabbits, timid brown people, made pop-guns of elder and collected stones for bullets.

THEN, under Hedgehog's directions, they dragged branches of prickly furze to the Roman road. The squirrels bent the slender hazel saplings into bows and filled their little fur pockets with arrows. The hedgehogs sharpened their quills and stood ready with all their own armour on their backs. Wise Owl flew over the woods, silent as a shadow, keeping watch and ward. Robin the Postman had a bow and a sheath of feathered arrows. The Speckledy Hen and her husband the Red Cock came armed with their sharp beaks and spurs.

INSIDE GREY RABBIT'S HOUSE all was bustle and stir. Hare ran upstairs and downstairs calling: " Grey Rabbit! Where's my catapult? Grey Rabbit! Where's my haversack? Grey Rabbit! Where's my helmet? Where's my red coat? Where's my umbrella? Where's my pistol? Make me some sandwiches of egg and watercress, Grey Rabbit."

Squirrel was knitting so fast she used eight needles at once.

Little socks and mittens and helmets fell to the floor as she made them, and she broke off the wool and started another garment.

"WHAT are all these things for?" asked Hare, kicking a mitten.

"Ammunition, I think," replied Squirrel, clicking her eight needles and knitting and purling at a great rate.

Hare slipped a woollen helmet over his head and pulled on a pair of gloves.

"Very comforting when I go to explore the North Pole," said he. "I expect Wise Owl would like a pair of socks, Squirrel."

"I'VE MADE HIM a nightcap," muttered Squirrel. "He lost his in the wash. Knit one, purl one, take seven together."

Little Grey Rabbit sewed a Red Cross on her blue apron. She tore up a sheet for bandages, and she packed a pin-cushion with thorns for pins. She fetched her ointments and her cures for all hurts from the corner cupboard, and she brewed some herb tea ready for the wounded. She made some sticking-plaster with the sweet gum of the larch-trees, and she put a bottle of violet smelling-salts in her bag.

HARE strutted up and down with his catapult. On his head he wore a saucepan, and covering his chest was a dish-cover. He carried his gas-mask on his back, and round his waist was a belt which held an ancient toy pistol he once found.

" I'm off to face the foe," he cried. " Tootle-too!" He played a tune on his trumpet and beat the dish-cover like a drum.

" Why do you want a butterfly net?" asked Grey Rabbit.

" That's a gas-mask," said Hare proudly. " My own invention. I shall wear it when Fuzzypeg throws the old-laid eggs at the Weasels."

"TOO-WHIT!   TOO-WHOO!"
called Wise Owl in a long-drawn
cry. "Too-whoo-oo-oo-oo! Get to
your places. They are coming near.".
An army of Weasels was marching
along the old grass-covered Roman
road. Their teeth shone white, their
noses were raised, their little fierce
eyes looked here and there, as their
long thin bodies moved swiftly over
the ground.

"GREY RABBIT lives over there," said the leader. "Hare and Squirrel live with her. We will eat them all up and live in their house. Then we will eat all the rabbits and squirrels and hedgehogs and mice in the country. They are kind, gentle animals and they will never dare to resist us. No, not one of them will fight. They don't even know we are coming. They will get a surprise when we enter their pleasant land. It will be as easy as winking to catch them all."

MOLDY WARP was working furiously at a trench which cut the old road. Deeper and deeper he went, and a band of rabbits with wheelbarrows were piling the soil high.

"What are you making?" whispered Hare, leaning over the trench to look at Mole.

"An ambush," muttered Moldy Warp.

"A hambush!" echoed Hare, and he walked off to find Grey Rabbit and Squirrel.

"Mole's making an egg-bush," said he. "No, a hambush. Ham and eggs for the Weasels," he explained.

AT LAST the deep trench was finished, and the animals threw their sharp thorns and furze bushes over the bottom of the long pit. Across the top they spread a layer of twigs, so delicately placed that they would snap with the lightest touch. Squirrels dropped grasses over the gap, and Robin the Postman came with a mail-bag full of leaf letters to sprinkle there.

"A ham-and-egg bush," whispered Hare to any one who had time to listen.

"AN AMBUSH," corrected Mole. "A trap to catch the enemy. Now hide yourselves with your pop-guns and don't move a whisker," he told the rabbits.

"Squirrels, all of you climb the trees and wait with your bows and arrows."

So the squirrels climbed the trees and the little rabbits hid in the bushes, with their pop-guns pointing towards the pit in the lane. They were shaking with excitement; they couldn't keep their whiskers from trembling.

T HEN LITTLE GREY RABBIT came up with the Red Cross on her apron, and her ointments and lollipops in her basket.

" Courage," she whispered. " Courage," and at once the little rabbits ceased trembling and their whiskers were still. They felt as brave as lions when they saw Grey Rabbit and heard her clear, soft voice.

FUZZYPEG and his cousins were crouched behind some dock-leaves, and in the nettle-bed beside them were the old-laid eggs.

"Throw your bombs in the trench when the Weasels fall into it," said Moldy Warp. "Be ready with your bombs and throw them at the enemy."

FUZZYPEG NODDED, and his cousins, Tim and Bill Hedgehog, seized the bad eggs and jigged with excitement.

" Be careful," warned Fuzzypeg. " If you wriggle like that you'll drop the eggs and we shall be gassed. Don't you remember how Rat's present of an old-laid egg knocked over all the small animals?"

The little Hedgehogs blushed and wriggled, and then, as Fuzzypeg frowned, they kept as still as their shaking prickles would allow them.

SQUIRREL came running up with a bundle of garments under her arm. She tossed them to the waiting rabbits, and they muffled their feet in gloves and mittens. They took up their bows and arrows, their pop-guns and cudgels, and lay in wait.

"Where's the army? Are they lost?" the animals asked each other; but once again Moldy Warp cried, "Hist! Never a word! Never a sound from any of you till I cry 'Fire'!"

Pitter-patter, pitter-patter, went the tiny muffled feet of all the little rabbits and squirrels and field mice and hedge-hogs as they crept back to their places.

TRAMP! TRAMP! went the feet of the Weasels down the green lane towards Grey Rabbit's house. Their long bodies moved in snaky columns as they followed their leader.

Suddenly Wise Owl dropped like a stone and carried off the big Weasel at the front of the army.

The rest squealed in surprise and hesitated. Those at the back marched on and the foremost were pushed on the thin layer of twigs over the pit. Down they went, one on top of another, falling head over heels into the ambush Mole had made. At the bottom of the pit were the thorns like a bed of spears to prick them.

"FIRE! FIRE!" shouted Moldy Warp, and bang went his old blunderbuss among them! A shower of little arrows and a hail of little stones fell among the scrambling Weasels. Then Fuzzypeg and Tim and Bill Hedgehog threw the old-laid eggs. Every egg hit a Weasel and knocked over a dozen others. Pouf! What a smell there was!

Hare put on his gas-mask and fired his sandwiches from his catapult by mistake. It wasn't until his haversack was empty that he discovered his mistake.

"JUST MY LUCK," he murmured. "Excellent egg-and-cress sandwiches all gone! And I've got stones to eat."

The Weasels struggled and fought and rolled about in the pit.

"A trap!" they cried, and they climbed on each other's backs and scrambled out.

SQUIRREL RACED out of their way, but she dropped her knitting as she ran. The eight needles stuck in the ground like spears, and the wool got twisted in the bushes and tangled in the thorns. Into it ran the Weasels. Their feet were caught and they fell.

"A NET to hold us!" they cried. "A net! It's the gamekeeper's snare!" They gave loud cries of terror and turned back. They ran as fast as they could, with Wise Owl darting down and seizing them, and Mole firing his old blunderbuss, and Hare waving his saucepan, and Squirrel shaking a half-knitted sock.

AWAY THEY WENT, over the fields, across the woods, many a mile to their own wild country.

"We will never go to Grey Rabbit's house again," they told each other as they licked their wounds and crept into their holes. "Never! The fiercest animals on earth live near Grey Rabbit's house."

ON THE BATTLE-FIELD Grey Rabbit attended to the wounded. She put bandages round the rabbits' paws and pinned them with thorns.

MRS. HEDGEHOG carried bowls of hot pea-soup to the tired little animals, and Old Hedgehog came hurrying up with a can of warm milk.

"I rolled like a ball all the way to the meadow where our Daisy was feeding. So I borrowed a pail from the dairymaid and milked the cow, and here's a sup for some of you," said he.

"WHERE'S MOLDY WARP, our leader? Where's Fuzzypeg, our bomber? Where's Wise Owl, our scout?" they asked.

Down the lane came Moldy Warp and Fuzzypeg, and behind them a crowd of little rabbits and hedgehogs and mice.

"YOU SHALL ALL COME to the feast of victory," promised Mole. " You have been as brave as anybody. Now the war is over and the Weasels have been defeated we needn't fear them any more."

"A FEAST?" cried Hare. "Ah! That's better! That's worth fighting for!" "Hurrah for Moldy Warp the leader!" cried the little army.

"Hurrah for little Fuzzypeg the bomber! Hurrah for Grey Rabbit the Red Cross nurse, and Squirrel the knitter and Hare the Home Guard!"

"COURAGE! FIGHT FOR FREE-DOM," they all sang, and Grey Rabbit wrote the words on the great oak tree which grew by the Roman road, so that they would always remember.

THE END